Seasonal
SHORTS

These Christmas-inspired stories and poems are the perfect quick read!

From old romantics to comedy to blood-curdling horror, and from tales of Santa's pants to those of neighbourly love, this well-rounded seasonal anthology is sure to contain something you'll love.

And the best bit? Many of the stories are flash fiction, meaning they can be read in just a couple of minutes or less, so you can fit in a quick read on your lunch break or in the queue at the store.

26 stories, written by 16 authors from Preston, UK, Seasonal Shorts is our gift to you at Christmas. Which will be your favourite?

Please note, some of the stories are not suitable for children under 12 due to their potentially scary nature or very occasional use of language.

Let's begin!

Contents

Gingerbread Season

by Leanne Dempsey

If I were a gingerbread man I would…

Avoid Greggs. At all costs.

That was where my mother and father went one snowy Saturday morning. We were all together in a row, warming nicely by a bread oven. My legs had tanned to a nice golden brown, and my baker gave me two purple buttons for my waistcoat. As we looked around, my father told me stories about the adventures of the snowflakes that were now gathering in crowds on the bakery window ledges. He spoke of all the distant lands they had visited, and their night equivalents the winter stars, which would shine upon us and a nice travelling fellow called Santa in a few hours' time.

But a night under the stars was not to be. Big hands shrouded us in darkness and when I opened my eyes again, I could see I was all alone.

I sat up, terrified, and called out for my family. A muffled moan replied. Out of the wide doors in the distance floated box after box, the moans descending from each one. The moans of my fellow gingerbread folk. The moans perhaps also of my parents!

I climbed down from my perch – it was high and I lost a few crumbs but there was no time to lose. I dodged a heavy pair of marching boots and hid until the coast was clear. Then I dashed across the floor, skidding on its slippery surface, my feet beginning to get soggy and lose their shape. I narrowly missed being biscuit dust as I got through the door before it slammed shut. Panting, I looked up. The cold air of the outside world hit me and I saw that this outside world was bigger than I ever imagined.

Wait! There was the last box. I shouted to it, and a muffled moan from my mother returned my call. I marched towards it, but suddenly the box launched into the air. Into a dark cave on wheels it went, and the cave door shut. A hum began and the screech of tyres sounded. I squinted to see the kidnapper. All I could see were big letters G – R – E – G – G – S on a white baker's hat floating away. I could hear the moans, the moans of my dear gingerbread, up until the end of the street, and then they were gone.

Old Friends

by Janice Cumberlidge

The doorbell rang, but we weren't expecting anyone, I mean, it was Christmas morning after all.

I pulled back the curtain an inch to see who it was and saw a woman in a Santa outfit, bending down to fix her rather short Santa skirt. As she lifted her head, I realised who it was. But surely not… Stacey? Here? On Christmas day?

My first reaction was of joy. It had been almost six years since I'd seen my best friend from high school.

But then I shuddered.

The boy.

Her boyfriend.

My now-husband.

I heard the front door open and raced towards it like I could somehow stop it happening.

But it was too late.

Stacey was standing face-to-face with the man I'd stolen from her. But she wasn't alone. To her side stood a little boy, holding her hand.

"Hello, Josh. Long time no see," Stacey said to my husband, glancing down the hall in my direction afterwards. "Oh, Maria, hi," she said, sounding disappointed.

"Hi," I managed to utter back, fearing the worst was yet to come.

"I believe this one belongs to you," she said, holding out the child's hand to Josh.

"Daddy, I made a snowman but I got lost and Mrs. Christmas found me and bringed me back!" the boy exclaimed.

"But…"

Josh was almost speechless. And so was I.

"How did I know he was yours?" Stacey preempted.

Josh nodded slowly.

"There's not much I don't know," she said, then turned to leave with a tear in her eye.

The Last Christmas

by Persis Peters

Her bones ached, her hair was in knots and it was late.

The veg was chopped, the turkey was thawing and she breathed a sigh of relief as the ink dried on the last gift tag of the evening. Time for bed. But something was missing. The last place she wanted to go was the loft but she'd forgotten the Christmas stockings. She tip-toed silently along the hallway, avoiding the usual creaky floor board and eased down the ladder, careful to make sure the scrape of the cold hard metal was inaudible as the children slept.

She hated Christmas. She was only 12 years old, an only and lonely child, on that Christmas morning when the police came to the front door. She had fallen into the knitted cocoon of her father's festive jumper as the policemen's words became nothing but white noise that ripped through her hot tears. Mum had popped out to fetch Grandma and her seasonal contribution of a truck's worth of sprouts. They had been banished from the Christmas table ever since. Bloody sprouts, and her pursuit of the perfect Christmas, had taken her mother's life in an instant. The driver was hung-over from Christmas Eve reverie. Desperate not to miss his Christmas dinner and disappoint his family, he had been rubbing his weary eyes when he didn't see her mother step onto the crossing. It would be funny if it wasn't so tragic. The ubiquitous over-cooked sprouts, by all accounts, had exploded on impact and at first no-one was quite sure if the sticky, deep red contents of Grandma's dusty bottle of sherry from the cabinet had slipped from her hand and joined the remainder of the green veg on the crossing. In fact Grandma was stood like stone, the sherry intact and gripped firmly in her frail hand, very much alive as she watched her daughter slip away.

With one shaky foot on the ladder and a wish for it to be January, when all of this charade would be over, she hauled herself into the rafters and thought of the kids. She did it for them; year after year, after year.

She was slowly backing out of the hatch when the tiniest glint from an object, caught by the hall lights below, drew her attention. The object belonged to something that had fallen from a box of long-forgotten history, clearly disturbed by earlier efforts to drag down the Christmas Tree from some far-flung corner of this abyss. She

3

allowed the stockings to float softly to the hallway floor as she reached into the dark space beyond, guided by the glow from the mystery item. She sat on the edge of the loft hatch, impatient with curiosity, and swept away decades of dust from a diary she didn't recognise, secured by a fragile and tarnished lock with its key still loosely guarding its secrets. The box that had been its keeper was labelled 'Mum'.

She flicked through the diary's pages, hungry for memories of her mother's soft voice and her elegant old-time handwriting that had graced every shopping list and Christmas card, when those little things were still taken for granted. There was nothing secret about it really. Notes scrawled in margins; reminders to pay the milkman and so on. Parents' evenings and birthdays got a mention but other than that, it was completely unremarkable apart from the unexpected lump it brought to her throat and the reminder that she had travelled those subsequent difficult years alone, caring for her father as he grew pale and shattered. She resented him for it. She flicked to the very end, just to be sure there was no unlikely earth-shattering family secret revealed within its pages, when an envelope, tucked in where Christmas Day had been left blank, leapt from between the leaves as they fluttered by. The envelope was yellowed at the edges and, although clearly never opened, its gummed seal had given way to the dried out, ages-old dust. She returned to the front cover of the diary. It was the year her mother had been taken. There was no account of Christmas Day because her mother had never seen the end of it but the page for that date had seemed to serve as a reminder that the envelope and its contents were to be shared then. In faded Biro she could just make out her own name. She could hear the smile in her mother's voice as she whispered the letter's contents to herself in the dimly lit hole above her hallway.

"My Beautiful Girl,

I have a very special gift for you this Christmas. It is something you have wanted for a long time. Before I tell you what it is, I have to say just how very proud of you I am. I worried, because I'm your Mum, that going to 'big school' would be such a change for you and you would find it a challenge like anyone else but you have taken it in your stride and I can see what a wonderful, caring, intelligent and special young lady you are turning out to be. Never forget though, you will always be my baby and it's important you understand that. You are old enough now to know that another baby will not change how I feel about you and I just know that you will be the best big sister ever. Happy Christmas my lovely girl; you will soon be able to tell everyone that a baby brother is on his way to keep you company.

I'll be with you when you open this letter and ready for a hug. Just you and me on Christmas night while Dad is sleeping off Grandma's sprouts.

Love always

Your Mum".

With her heart thumping and aching for memories that had never been, knowing her father's loss was so much greater than she had known, she gripped the ladder for support as she dropped silently to the hallway floor. She had become nothing and nobody over the years; a silhouette living in the shadow of what could have been but something stirred inside her. She looked in on her beautiful girls, their tired and over-excited faces resting and dreaming of tomorrow, and thanked the universe for these gifts that she had taken for granted. She carried her love for them down the stairs, through to the kitchen and picked up her phone. The text to their father read, 'Bring sprouts', as she prepared to be wonderful and make everything special again.

Naughty or Nice

by Matthew Bennett

It was Christmas Eve and snow covered every inch of ground in this nameless town. Flakes piled upon flakes and balanced themselves on slender branches like circus performers.

Tonight the town was happy, tonight the town was asleep. Adults dreamed their perverted dreams and children dreamed their dreams of innocence and toys... but not everyone was sleeping, not tonight.

In a big house on the very edge of town there was one little boy who was still awake. His name was Timmy, and he and his stuffed friend Teddy were currently hiding beneath their bed. The mattress above them was still wet from Timmy's little accident. That little accident was the reason that he wasn't calling out for his parents right now, they didn't like his little accidents at all. Timmy was a big boy and big boys didn't do that sort of thing. Timmy couldn't help himself though, not when he had seen that face at the window. That face that was not jolly at all. Not one little bit.

Timmy lay as still as he could and listened to the sounds coming from behind the walls of his room. The creaking and cracking of plasterboard and wood. The breathing and the whispers. Right now, Timmy was more frightened then he had ever been, even more so than that time he had glued Susan's lips shut. When he'd been waiting at school for his parents to pick him up and take him home and punish him, he'd nearly wet himself then too. He'd been braver that time though, much braver.

Timmy looked deep into Teddy's eyes.

"I wish that you were big enough to look after me."

Teddy didn't answer, Teddy was scared too.

There came a dull thump from the hall outside his bedroom door and Timmy jumped. He was here, that face was inside the house. Floorboards creaked, growing louder and louder. Closer and closer. Then, the creaking stopped and a whisper slipped through the gap below his bedroom door.

"Timmy. Timmy. You've been a very bad boy."

Poor Timmy could only watch as his bedroom door slowly swung open, revealing a pair of big, black, dirty boots. It was all that Timmy could see of the figure but he wished that he could see less. Much less. With Teddy clutched to his chest he slid as far back away from the boots as he could.

He heard a deep laugh.

The boots approached Timmy's wet bed. A red, bearded face, the eyes hidden behind shadows, came into view. Timmy could only stare and Timmy could only watch as a gloved hand reached out towards him.

Timmy felt his pyjamas grow wet again.

"Merry Christmas, Timmy..."

Santa's Pants

by Leanne Dempsey

"Mrs. C! Are you there?
Where ARE they? Can't find them anywhere!"

He sat back, rubbed his head
-His red jacket still lay slumped on the bed.
He was going to shout again at the top of his voice
When she replied sternly to stop making ALL THAT NOISE
("and wherever you last had them, they'll be there!")

The man of the house threw an exasperated look.
It was no use. He couldn't trace the red spotty ones that brought him luck.
His trousers he heaved on
And the red suit of make-believe thrust upon;
He gave the missus a hug
Tripped over the rug
Then to the reindeer shed he was gone.

"Come on lads! Come on Dasher! Get out of bed!
-Now where did I put the keys to the sled?"
Mr. C hurried off, moustache askew
To start his new motor. And, right on cue,
The deer filed out, yawning.
Wondering why the boss liked so early a morning.

First he reversed the sled over Rudolph's hoof
Then he mistimed the thrust and hit the porch roof.
In a cloud of dust ten minutes later
All reindeer were assembled and he hit the accelerator.
"I'm sure I'll be fine without my lucky Y-fronts!"

He said, with his trousers on back to front.

Russia was first on his delivery list
But he got a bit lost, must have missed
The turning. Ah well, thought he.
It's full of forests and I'm still only learning.
(At the ripe young age of one hundred and three)

So the leader of Russia missed a present or two.
Onto America to deliver a few.
This was Mrs C's favourite place, but for her husband this wasn't the case.
He lost a reindeer out in Area Fifty One
And sent the 'how to be president' kit to Trump, not Clinton.
Boys got dolls, girls got Lego bricks
They thought maybe Santa hadn't had his Weetabix.

The sweltering Caribbean got bobble hats and mitts,
While Iceland got bikinis and barbecue kits.
Florida got oranges – as if they hadn't enough
Meanwhile in Brazil, Santa caught his cuff
On Christ the Redeemer
Tearing his coat from this slight misdemeanour.
("A big man? On a hill?! How long has THAT been there, Brazil??")

In Africa he flew too low; the reindeers protested – onward they would not go
After being chased by lions. They said they'll stick to snow.
In London, Santa had particular crisis
Meandering all the bridges and he narrowly missed
The one with the towers. Down into the Thames plunged the sleigh
The reindeers, soaked, decided they would lead the way.
Homeward bound before he ruins the day!

But not yet, Santa thought. We need to get these toys

To Norway to their dear girls and boys.
It won't take long! Famous last speeches.
He fell down a Norwegian chimney, burnt his bottom and his breeches.
They arrived back at the North Pole port
Burnt, bitten, bruised and a reindeer short
(Also with a leftover sack of candy)
—Santa blamed it all on no lucky seasonal shorts.
….Mrs. C put it down to too much brandy.

And not Mrs. C nor Rudolph nor Dasher dared to say
Was: "Santa, it's not even Christmas Day!"
It was actually only December 21.
Ah well. They didn't want to spoil Santa's fun.

The Twelve New Days of Christmas

by Nicholas McDonald

"This is a nightmare!" Liz Turnpike exclaimed in despair. "The show is on in twenty minutes! What is happening?"

This was her big break as a director, and at the age of 26, she knew it had come very early, so she was eager to please the television executives with her live performance of the *Twelve Days of Christmas*, but, like all plans, nothing goes according to it.

"Explain this to me again, Mark." She sat down at her desk, then as just as quickly stood to her feet. "We have twelve drummers, yes?"

"Yes."

"But they don't have any drums?"

"That is true."

She stared Mark in his nervous eyes, and admired him for trying to remain sprightly, but she could see though his act. He had only just entered his twenties and similar to her, he wanted to impress, however, those he relied on had let him down and he knew he had to face the brunt of it.

"So how are they going to drum?"

"Well, ermm… Do they need to?"

"The line is, twelve drummers *drumming*. Oh wow. And the pipers?"

Mark looked to the floor in embarrassment.

"And the pipers, Mark? What about them?"

"This is my error. At the time you asked me to get the pipers to pipe I thought you had a misunderstanding of the technical term for that certain career."

She stared at him blankly, her fingers scratching into the surface of her desk.

"You see," Mark continued, "I didn't get pipers to pipe… I got plumbers."

She slumped into her chair, her head buried into her hands. Mark couldn't quite hear her, but Liz was muttering to herself, but he guessed whatever she was saying, it didn't sound very Christmassy.

Liz stood from her desk and marched out of the room, dreading what was happening on stage without her. Mark followed and she asked him to inform her of the rest of the cast, hoping things couldn't get worse. For a moment they didn't, as he confirmed that they did in fact have ten Lords a leaping *and* nine ladies dancing, although Alex Simkins helped out with that one, so the nine ladies where scantily dressed. The eight maids had been replaced with farmers since, as time has gone by, milking cows had probably disappeared from the job specifications of a maid.

"And the geese?" Liz asked as she entered the theatre, only for her find out the answer to that herself, as seven ducks flapped and quacked around on stage, Emily doing her best to keep them in order, but failing.

"Ducks?" She looked at Mark with fierce eyes, but he was pretending to read his notebook. "And the gee-"

"Chickens. But they are laying."

"This is incredible. We're re-writing a classic to perform live on TV. Great! What's your back-up career, Mark?"

Mark didn't hear her question, he was distracted with the next bit of bad news he had to deliver, but he had lost the guts to say it, so instead, he removed the contents of his pocket, one at a time.

"Here's the next one, Liz." He took out a gold ring a placed it in her hand "You're better off looking after them." He placed a second, a third, then a fourth, and finally… his Grandma's silver wedding ring.

"What's this?"

"It's my Grandma's wedding ring. She said we can borrow it for the show."

"But why? Why are you using you're Grandma's wedding ring."

Mark coughed in attempt to clear his throat.

"I-I ermm, I… misplaced it…" He trailed off, cowering like a terrified puppy. He knew he was riding his luck and was surprised Liz hadn't murdered him yet, but when he looked at her, he could see she was angry, but instead chuckling to herself."

"Obviously, you've misplaced a Golden Ring. Let's replace it with a Haribo one, shall we?"

"Really?"

She rolled her eyes and strolled along the aisle until she got to the stage and saw four tough-looking women, who must have come from the rough side of town.

"And these are who, exactly, Mark?"

"I didn't know what calling birds were so Alex Simkins said he'd help me out with it, he knew a few people. But he said I was being a bit sexist, they're not called birds, they're girls, whatever he meant by that."

Just then Alex Simkins appeared on the stage and winked at one of the girls. They all waved teasingly and simultaneously said "Hi, Alex."

"So, what do you think? You're welcome, Mark." Alex spoke with a deluded arrogance.

"Call girls? Really?" Liz replied.

"Yeah, that's what you wanted, right?"

"Keep walking, Alex. Trust me, keep walking."

And he did, but not without a chorus of "Bye, Alex."

She looked around the stage and saw three French hens, but Mark assured her, that with all the talk of Brexit and leaving the EU, that the audience might not like foreign hens, so recommended calling them British hens. She laughed, but still agreed. Liz had decided to embrace the chaos, after all, it was Christmas, and the situation had gotten so out of hand there was nothing left for her to do, except get on with it and enjoy whatever catastrophe was shown on live TV, and probably ruin her reputation for good.

A delivery man appeared on stage with two turtles and two doves, to which Mark explained that he searched in the furthest corners of the world but was unable to find a turtle and dove hybrid, and no scientist could make him one, let alone two at such short notice. Liz decided it was best not to inform him of his misunderstanding. And finally, with hope of a long forgotten commodity, she inquired about the Partridge.

"I couldn't rent a Partridge, but I did get this." He walked across the stage to a bookshelf, revealing the *Alan Partridge: Nomad* book. "I thought we could stick this in the tree, as an okay alternative."

Liz was in stunned silence. She looked up to the sky, shut her eyes, and then walked quietly off the stage.

The audience gathered, and the cameras were on… Action!

And there was a lot of action too; the ducks quacked, the lords leaped, the plumbers pirouetted with their pipes as the drummers hummed. The chickens did lay, as the call girls recognised and waved to a few clients in the audience, to their embarrassment (and their spouses anger). The British hens drew cheers from the Patriotic, and as the silver ring was dropped through a crevice in the stage, Mark's jawed dropped in pure terror; the farmers milked their cows, causing a few of the pirouetting plumbers and leaping lords to slip on the milk. The turtles and doves remaining moved little and finally the cast danced around the tree, into which Alan Partridge's book was wedged.

As they sang the final chorus, Liz was crying, but with laughter, causing Mark to also laugh, and Alex, until Liz slapped him around the back of the head and told him to get lost. The choir sang the song perfectly:

12 drummers humming,
11 plumbers piping,
10 Lords a leaping,
9 Ladies dancing,
8 farmers a milking,
7 ducks a swimming,
6 chickens a laying,
1 silver and foooour gold rings,
4 call girls,
3 British hens,
2 turtles and doves,
And Alan Partridge's book in a tree.

The audience loved it and the viewings went sky high, as Liz was labelled the Queen of Christmas satire. She appreciated the title, but assured everyone that it was a team effort, and that Mark played a huge part in the re-writing of the *Twelve New Days of Christmas*.

Christmas Eve

by Maya Anna Ozolina

In our house we celebrate Christmas Eve, that's an old Latvian tradition.

As every year, I'm ready for it. To be lucky, happy, or at least alright all year till the next Christmas we need at least seven, even better nine, different dishes on the festive table. I'm ready for that as well.

There are several birds, fish and vegetables happily cooking, roasting, baking, frying and simmering away on my wood burning stove.

It is hot in here, really roasting. I have to get out, at least for a while, before my senses burn out. I grab my coat and quietly, so as not to disturb the family, shy away through the kitchen door.

It's fresh, cool, dark and all white outside. I suddenly feel an overwhelming joy. I love walking; I can walk for miles. So I walk and walk, forgetting all about the roasting, baking, cooking and simmering things in my kitchen. Freedom!

I reach a quiet, remote spot. Suddenly I hear strange noises, like small feet stamping on the crisp snow. I stop, but it's too dark to see anything. I go closer to the source of the sounds.

There are a few snowmen standing in a circle. They are still, but their heads are nodding towards each other in a slow rhythm. I freeze.

The biggest snowman says in a hoarse voice, "We have to make the final decision, should we be nice to humans tonight or scare them to death? Please vote now."

I freeze even more, if that's possible. "Oh, thank you, you just have executed the second option, without any consent from your fellow snowmen!"

I'm glad I didn't say that out loud, you know, just in case!

I silently address myself. "Most likely, it's time to turn around, surrender and go back home."

Well, if I'm brutally honest with myself, I really should *not* sip that whisky between preparing the seventh and ninth dishes.

The Christmas Altruist

by Arthur Chappell

I always said that if I won the lottery, I would use the money to help the needy rather than spending it all on me. Like most people, I resented those who won £10 million or more and just indulged in endless spending. I reckon anyone could retire comfortably on half a million in personal savings.

My thinking changed when my numbers came up, and it became almost literally time to put my money where my mouth was.

It wasn't just a big win, but the biggest ever. The World Lottery had been growing for five months of rollovers through no winning combinations coming up and incredibly, two unclaimed wins as well. I claimed my prize as soon as I got over the shock of realising my ticket matched the balls.

I quit my call centre job right away, treating my dozen co-workers to two million between them, so they quit too.

After a month long holiday and buying myself a swanky New York apartment, I settled to the question of what to really do with my virtually unlimited wealth. My interest was going sky high and my mail was now ninety-percent begging letters. I hired two secretaries and a team of shredders to deal with my correspondence. They were my first employees. My accountant was next, followed by a top grade lawyer. Managing my money was becoming a business. I was turning into a manager, a CEO, a fat cat.

Christmas was looming, so I wanted to do something really altruistic for the children of the World. I had the potential to be a real-life Father Christmas. My first thought was a toy for every child on the planet. Realism quickly kicked in on that notion. Science wasn't up to creating gravity defying reindeer and no single vehicle from sled to 747 could carry enough toys for every under ten on Earth.

Then there was a question of real needs. The famine in the Sudan was generating a TV appeal. There were many heart-breaking shots of kids with their ribs hanging out and swollen tongues. They didn't need toys but food and water. I started planning for welfare distribution.

It became a logistical nightmare from the outset. I needed fleets of trucks and aircraft and thousands of staff. I wasn't a manager any more but a mogul. I also ran into government opposition both at home and abroad, so I was now employing political advisors and ambassadors, PR people, etc. I had factories, and established my own call centres to handle queries from those affected by and concerned by my activity, hiring people to the very kind of work I had fled on winning the big one.

Rebels and counter-rebels alike started attacking my food convoys, so I bought in a team of military advisors and even hired a few mercenaries to protect the supplies—I now had an army. I was an international arms dealer.

My wealth was turning me into the very kind of capitalist I hoped to escape from through my betting. My ulcers were generated by my increasing stress levels, said the finest medics I could buy myself.

Many hated me for my determination to do good for the World. I was putting many charities out of business. I had to accept competition when I was sued for monopolising the markets. I was accused of trying to buy myself everything from knighthoods to canonisation. I had enemies and I needed bodyguards. I survived two attempts at assassination. I have the wealth of Bruce Wayne but without the powers to be Batman. I am as rich as Croesus, so why do I feel so lonely, like I was the poorest man on Earth?

Seasonal Shorts

by Janice Cumberlidge

It was cold out, snow fleeting past the window, swirling and gathering in drifts by the garden hedges. Derek was glad he'd come home from work early and didn't have to go out again until Monday if he didn't want to.

He pulled open his tie, kicked off his brogues, and poured himself a glass of single malt whiskey. Only Fools and Horses was playing on the box—the Christmas special of course—and the sofa provided a comforting relief after being stuck in meetings all day, sat bolt upright in the unforgiving, one-size-fits-all office chairs.

Derek roared with laughter as Del Boy and Rodney entertained, and the drink certainly helped loosen him up. But there was still something missing.

Placing the drink on the side table, Derek got up and went out to the hallway. He whacked the heating on full blast and started upstairs.

Rummaging at the back of the wardrobe, his hand landed on exactly what he was looking for.

Five minutes later, Derek sat back down on the sofa, feeling more relaxed than ever. He made a mental note not to answer the doorbell that night, this was his time.

Derek looked down and smiled. His red, flashing reindeer underpants and fluffy snowman slippers were just the ticket.

O Christmas Tree

by Mandy Pang

"Well I guess this is me then, wish me luck."

Poor thing. For a tree so tall and magnificent, he looks positively terrified. Still, they look like a nice family, and he's going to a good home. I feel the others breathe a sigh of relief, their bristles relaxing a little. The biggest and best of us has been picked. We others are now in with a chance.

It's fascinating, watching the humans. Some of them have that slightly mad look in their eyes. Their need to find the perfect tree to set the scene for a the perfect Christmas. They touch, they smell, they walk round and round, sizing up my dimensions, my symmetry, judging if I am the right shade of green, the appropriate fullness and height that they are looking for. I just stand there, and try not to take it all too personally. I do my best to appear as proud and Christmas Tree-ish as I can. I see how some of the other trees lean forward so the humans will notice them. I cant bring myself to do it, I don't want to come across as desperate.

Four days till Christmas and I begin to grow bored, anxious and tired. I can tell my bristles are beginning to turn brown and I feel so dry. The spotty, deep-voiced teenager who works on the weekend is busy chatting up girls and neglecting his duties. I haven't been pruned or watered for over a week now. Being one of the last ones left, I expect I look pretty pathetic.

*

I can't believe I've left it so late. I'm a terrible mother. There's still the presents to wrap, stockings to fill and Jack's Christmas jumper to knit. And what on earth possessed me to volunteer to throw a party on Christmas Eve? God, I'm stressed. The customer service here is absolutely terrible. I feel like I'm going to burst into tears. And I want to throttle that spotty teenager. Who has the time to stand around chatting people up? I have exactly 15 minutes to pick a tree before I battle the hell that is Asda for the final Christmas shop.

"Mummy, I like this one."

I look at Jack, and he's staring up in awe at one of the very few trees left and I just melt. Walking towards the tree, my heart sinks. I take a closer look. Sure its tall, it has a full bottom but it just looks, well… sad.

"Mummy, please?" Jack pleads. "It needs us, and we need it."

I look at my husband, and we both know this limp, pathetic looking tree is coming home with us.

*

They have placed me in the corner of their large living room, right in front of the window. I twinkle brightly at the passers by. I am adorned with handmade decorations and baubles. Multi coloured paper chains have been carefully wrapped around me. The house is completely silent, they will be waking up at any moment now.

"Merry Christmas, beautiful boy!"

"Merry Christmas, Mummy and Daddy!"

They hug, and I feel myself swell with pride and gratitude.

As they reach underneath me, and hand each other their carefully chosen gifts, I feel complete.

*

It's the New Year now and after weeks of being indoors, I enjoy the feeling of the sharp wind blowing through me. I don't know where I am going, and I have to admit, I am afraid. I have a lived a short, wonderful life, a Christmas full of laughter, love and family. Why does my time have to end now?

The boy is sobbing. He doesn't want to leave me. Everyday we have looked upon each other with awe and joy.

"Come on now sweet heart, its going to be alright."

His mum takes him by the hand as his dad gently unhooks me from the roof of their car.

This is it. My time has come to an end.

"What a beauty. I hope you enjoyed him?" A sturdy looking man with a big white beard and a cheerful voice greets the family.

"We couldn't have wished for a more wonderful tree."

"You've come just at the right time. Do you want to see?" The man is holding a spade, inviting them to watch.

I have become the Christmas tree that keeps on giving. I am a part of the beach here in Lytham, and in time I will form the sand dunes. I get to live anew, and live in hope that one day I will see the boy's face again.

Two Little Kittens

by Nusantara Banget-Rani

Dawn was in the air. The chirp of Winter birds made a beautiful choir across the hill, here in Christmas Tree village. It was the same in all the other nearby villages, but we believed this snowy hill with its green pine trees were the best in the Christmas valley.

A little boy, opening his big, dark green eyes, saw the sunrise shining through his bedroom window. The magenta light brought a sparkle to the glittering snow on the peaks and valleys of the distant mountains. He heard a sound, like tiny bells ringing, as snow dropped from the roof onto the window sill. Magic, he thought.

He got up from his tiny bed, went to the kitchen and took some of the pie his mother had prepared for his lunch later that day. He needed to go to Christmas town down in the valley soon. As a well-known road crossing sweeper in the area, he needed to be on time, especially at this time of year, when the weather would allow him to earn more money.

"Don't forget your hat," his mother reminded him after he got up from the old kitchen chair. The fire was blazing from the hearth and gave him hope for the day ahead. He put on the best coat he had on top of his scruffy waistcoat.

"Your hat!" his mom shouted again as he was heading towards the front door with his broom. He ran back towards her and kissed her forehead.

"Love you mum."

"Me too, sweetheart, try to stay warm!" But he had already banged the door shut, helped by the wind and snow that was dancing and swirling around.

He took a deep breath as he took the first step on the path covered with deep snow. The sun hid under thick, grey cloud and the snow chilled him through to his bones. He kept going, walking down the hill—what a dreadful day for Christmas Eve.

The gas lamp post and Christmas garland that the Acorn family had put out helped guide him along the path down to the valley. He was glad Mr. Old Owl's house was further up as it would not have helped him during the night—he did not have any Christmas decorations outside his house. His hot temper was getting worst after his wife's death too. No one dared mention Christmas to him. But it was quite hard for those who live here not to—our village's name is Christmas Tree village!

At last, he came to the end of the Curly-Wurly road and the last pine tree. He spotted a red and white dotted mushroom house and heard a Christmas song. The Christmas Bag Bubbles house shone from a far, and he heard laughter. He was relieved when Mrs. Orange Fox's grocery shop came in to view.

The Christmas valley is always busy at this time of year. Though it was already seven in the morning, the darkness still haunted. His post lay between Mrs. Orange Fox's grocery shop and the Grand Hotel, owned by the Grand Duke of Stars—he owned most of the Christmas Tree valleys.

Carts were loading and unloading fresh produce in the market in front of the hotel. The fishmonger had already created a fresh and smoky smell in the air. It competed with the smoke from the chimney of every building and a few cotton mills in town too.

He heard his first customer stop in front of him. The grand carriage made the last click-clock-clank sound on the muddy cobbled street. Straight away he ran a yard ahead with his broom and swept his best. The Grand Duke of Stars put down some coppers—more than he expected.

"How are you this morning young boy, have you written your list to Father Christmas?" The little boy smiled and bowed.

There were some who were generous enough to give him some copper for his pocket so he could help his mother at the end of the day with bread to take home. But the majority did not care, they didn't even pay for the service he gave.

He had written on his list to Father Christmas that he really wanted a kitten. They could not afford a very expensive one. He did not have any companions beside his mother and was often feeling lonely as he had no one to play with.

The night came at last and he did not want to stay out any longer. It was too dangerous, Mrs. Fox had said. He hopped on to one of the vegetable carts that would drop him near Christmas tree valley. He was happy could bring cakes, chutney and even bread home but there would be no turkey in his house for Christmas dinner tomorrow. He sighed.

As soon as he stepped into the woods, his sadness evaporated, and he was stunned by the glittering lights along the path—red, blue, yellow, green, golden sparks with colourful bubbles. Christmas Tree village was alive. From the Grand Duke of Stars' hotel, to Mrs. Robin's cottage, even Mr. Old Owl's tree house and his own small house were lit up.

He opened the door to share the news with his mom and another surprise was waiting for him. Everyone had squeezed into his small kitchen to greet him, including Mr. Old Owl, who smiled through his old spectacles.

It was the best Christmas Eve ever, he thought, as they ate dinner and the Grand Duke of Stars sang and danced. He even heard the bell ringing again after midnight but there was no snow—it was clear night. And then… ho ho ho. He opened his eyes as morning came.

"Christmas day!!!" he shouted. Then, he saw a rustle and heard a strange sound from the end of his bed.

"Meowww…."

A kitten? He jumped out of bed and saw *two* beautiful ginger cats. He cuddled them and rolled on the wooden floor with laughter. His mom came and the little boy gave her the tightest hug she'd ever experienced.

People from the hills and villages had helped his mother to buy the kittens, and the Grand Duke of Stars apparently played the biggest role.

"What names will you give them?" his mom asked.

"Bubble and Blossom." He smiled.

Think Twice at Christmas

by Karen Howarth

It was Christmas Eve. Kathleen Landy sat, trying not to shiver, in front of a small electric fire in her front room. It was the only room she lived in nowadays. She couldn't afford to heat the rest of the house, she couldn't even afford to use the oven. Condensation slowly ran down the bay windows, pooling on the windowsill. She could see her breath as she leaned forward to warm her hands. Then there was a knock at the door.

Kathleen hesitated. Cold callers, Jehovah's Witnesses, kids playing 'knock-a-door run'... they had all been round. She rubbed her hands together briskly, then showed her hands to the heat again. This time the doorbell rang followed by the sound of a woman's voice.

"Mrs. Landy... are you there? Is everything alright? Can you come to the door?"

She got up and shuffled along the hallway. She lifted the letterbox cover and looked out.

"Hello Mrs. Landy," said the lady on the other side, "you remember me? It's Cheryl from next door."

Cheryl was lovely. Cheryl was safe.

Kathleen lifted the latch and opened the door.

"Blimey, it's cold in there!"

Cheryl stepped inside and took Kathleen's wizened hands in hers.

"Oh sweetheart, your hands are freezing".

She rubbed them together, her wedding rings rattled but stuck fast at her knuckle. Cheryl stood in the ice palace that was Kathleen Landy's hallway and thought; this wasn't right. Something needed to be done. She grabbed Kathleen's coat and put it round her shoulders.

"Come on, can I have your keys?"

Kathleen took them out of her pocket and placed them in Cheryl's outstretched hand.

"Don't worry Mrs. Landy, let's get you in the warm and I'll put the kettle on."

Cheryl locked up the house and they slowly walked next door.

A wall of warmth met them as the front door opened. Kathleen found herself ensconced in front of the TV with a blanket around her shoulders. By the time Cheryl had returned with a cup of tea, she had fallen asleep. Cheryl went back in to the kitchen where her husband, Mick, was sitting at the table.

"Her house was freezing when I went round. I'm so worried about her. Can we have her stay for Christmas?"

Mick paused, "I think this is deeper than Christmas, love. Let me make some phone calls and enquire about any family she may have. We don't want to be stepping on anyone's toes.... but yes, let's have her for Christmas."

Cheryl went back to the living room to find Kathleen sipping her tea.

"Hello Kathleen, you were asleep before". As she sat down, Cheryl continued, "we were hoping you would accept our invitation to stay for Christmas".

A tear appeared in the corner of Kathleen's eye, "Oh, that would be lovely dear." She leaned back into the chair and sighed a heavy sigh. There were still good people in the world.

Dance With Me

by Susan Moffat

"Dance with me," he said, grabbing her waist and swinging her towards him.

The street was littered with the final few die hard clubbers, clutching cold kebabs and the optimistic belief that they could still get a cab.

"Dance with me," he said, "It's a beautiful night and I don't want it to end yet."

She laughed, "You're crazy. We'll get into trouble."

"No we won't. Come on. Relax a little. Dance with me!"

He took her hand, guiding her with him, twirling and gliding until the drunken wanderers stopped to watch them. Somewhere, from someone's phone, music began to play and he altered their rhythm to fit the seasonal tune.

"Stop," she giggled, "It's not appropriate and I'm not exactly dressed for dancing."

"Sod appropriate," he said, "I just want to have fun. And you look beautiful!"

The clear night sky was up-lit with the orange glow of the street lights and a slight frost was beginning to creep across the cobbled marketplace. Her feet slipped ungracefully in her rubber soled shoes. She laughed again.

"Happy New Year," he whispered, as his radio crackled.

"Happy New Year, Officer Clarke," she whispered back, "Now, let's get back to work."

Your Future in Presents

by Janice Cumberlidge

I was excited to open my Christmas present from Steve, we'd decided to buy each other something that symbolised our future.

I ripped the paper off in anticipation.

"A toy helicopter?"

I have no idea what I'm supposed to do with this.

Steve looks at me and grins.

"It's for your movie, the ones you said you'd make if you had the budget."

"So, err, the one in my story was…"

How do I put this without making him feel like a cheapskate?

"…much bigger than this. I mean, you'd be lucky to fit one of the cats in this thing. It doesn't exactly scream 'big-budget movie', does it?"

"Yeah but I was talking to a guy who does video productions and he says he can CGI it in, make it look like the real thing. He can do it, I'm sure."

***

Two months later, I'm sitting in a basement, holding onto my toy helicopter, dangling it from wires over a fish tank full of guppies pretending to be sharks, dipping Ken and Barbie into the water, with old 12" records of the theme from Jaws playing in the background.

Not quite the movie had in mind.

But then again, the microwaveable meal-for-one bowls were probably not what he had in mind either.

Captive at Christmas

by Sam Arthur

I have not been looking forward to this day. Many people do, but not I. I don't understand what there is to be excited about, who could possibly be excited about the eve of my Death?

I remember my young life so well now, sitting round with my own family. We would talk, take in the air, and just be happy with our lives. It was not a lot, but it was nice. That was before I was brutally removed from all that. I was sitting with my family, like I have always done, and these men came. Big men, brandishing great big saws, and in one fell swoop, they cut my feet off. I can still remember the cutting of the sharp blade on my achilles tendons. I screamed as loud as I could, begging these men, these Monsters; to stop, but they did not hear, probably enjoying my puppy dog whimpering. I was grabbed by the neck and dragged through the forest; the screams of family, friends and acquaintances ringing through the air. Eventually I was tossed in the back of a van, on top of others, packed in tight and deep, before being taken away from my once peaceful life.

I was taken to a big open caged area, where I was dropped off, my feet cemented in a wooden block, unable to move. The wounds to my ankles were still exposed, and I could feel each hit and niggle as I was played around like a sack of potatoes. And there I was made to wait. I was in pain, my legs throbbing; they treated the rest of my body more kindly as they spread my arms, hands and fingers out. They placed me with others like me; some from other parts of the world, and finally branded me with a coloured sticker, tightly bound round my neck. And there I was made to wait, wait for my turn.

My turn did not take long to come. I saw others before me go. Some were bigger; others smaller, but eventually my time came. A nice group of people came, big smiles of joy spread across their faces; picking me out like others. I hoped they would not; I was already in pain, and having seen what happened to everyone else, I did not want to go through that myself. But I had no choice; one of the big men came over, grabbed me by the neck, a tight grip round my throat, dragged me in the block, and pushed me into the tight tunnel. I could hardly breathe as I was pushed in, squashed together, and tied up in tight white netting. They removed the block at my feet. I could wriggle my feet a little, but then, they hacked at them once more; whittling tiny bits off at me with their tiny axe; each time cutting into my only shortly healed veins. Before I knew it, I had another, much tighter and thinner block on my feet. I was finally pulled out of the tunnel; tied, not gagged thankfully; before finally being bundled in the back of the family car, sold like a slave to be their prisoner.

When they brought me to my new home, the torture continued. As soon as they set me up and thankfully untied me, they bound bright colourful objects, even chocolate to my body; nearly cutting off the circulation to my wrists and fingers, binding them tightly. It was not just my ankles that began to throb, my arms, wrists and ankles, they all did. The cherry on the cake was a big shiny hat which thankfully was simply placed on my head, although they did have to cut off some of my hair to get it on.

That is where I have been since that day; standing still in a green block, my arms, wrists, hands and fingers still throbbing under the pain of the rope. They come in every now and then, light me up with some lights, putting me on display, giving joy to their family and friends, all marvelling at the family captive, sometimes even laughing at me too. They surrounded me with gifts, not for me you understand, for them, ones they can give to each other, while I just suffer with very little to eat.

I have heard stories from others of what will happen to me. It's the same for everyone. Once this day is over, I will soon turn brown, losing my lovely shade of green, my skin will fall off and I will just be a mass of bones, before I am finally laid to die in bits. I don't know how long it will be until that day, but I feel like it will be soon. There is no escape for me here; I know this is what will come of me. I barely have enough energy to move, let alone escape. They all sit there, with joy in their faces, dispensing presents between one another, gifts that I have had at my feet for a few days now. They look stuffed. I caught glimpses of the food they wasted on themselves, while I stand here, never sitting, always standing, with nothing but a tiny drip of water to sate my thirst.

I long for this day to be over, for soon I will be free. Not for long, I understand, but it should be all over soon.

A Snowman

by Maya Anna Ozolina

I am alone this Christmas and don't feel I deserve it.

On top of that, I missed the last train. I have a return ticket but no money. My phone is nearly dead, I don't have anyone to call and I don't have any friends or acquaintances in this small town. My chances of getting home are very slim, probably 0.01%.

To walk 9.5 miles in the snow on my own doesn't seem too exciting. In Summer, it would take three hours, but it is Winter now.

In different place and era, I might hitchhike. Now? Ha-ha!

I start to walk, and I'm glad I learned in my childhood how to take directions from the stars, and I'm glad there are plenty of them tonight.

I take a shortcut; I will be home before the morning, hopefully. But to what? That is the question.

It's getting colder and I'm tired. I need a break. With all this snow around that I enjoyed so much in my childhood, should I build a snowman?

Somehow suddenly it seems like a good idea.

I feel like I'm a child again. I roll up a body, head, arms and even legs, all white and crispy. I don't have the strength to lift the parts and put them on top of each other, so my snowman is lying down. He needs eyes and a mouth so I take two lucky pennies out of my pocket; here we go… eyes… now he can see.

I create a mouth, it's open; he looks a bit surprised now.

I am tired. This was a break. Shall I take a break from the break?

My snowman's eyes shine, he looks at me and a quiet voice says:

"Lay next to me, it will be warmer."

I am tired. Where I am going? I lay next to him. He feels freezing cold. I pull my knees towards my chest and wrap my arms around them in a foetus pose. Surprisingly it gets warmer indeed.

Will I be born again?

"You will", the snowman says.

I feel warmer and warmer, lighter and lighter.

Is this what happiness feels like?

I don't know.

I know nothing, I feel nothing and nothing is around.

Doctor Humbug

by Jake Trusler

Here he comes, the fat old git, thought Doctor Smith. The surgery door creaked open revealing a gormless old ball of cholesterol and burst capillaries. As the man stepped through the door, Smith stifled a sigh. He hated this part of the job. It wasn't so much the giving of bad news, but the dealing with a response from someone you already don't much care for.

"Sit down, Mr. Claus," he said reluctantly. He was enabling the man's delusions, but then, when someone changes their name, which he had to assume this bubble of Christmas spirit and undiagnosed mental disorders had done, there wasn't much a doctor could do. Confrontation was not part of the job description, and the Hippocratic oath meant that he really had to prioritise in this appointment.

"Afternoon, Doctor Smith, and a merry Christmas to you." Said the man, his mouth barely visible through the thicket of white fur he had clearly been cultivating for years. Smith wondered where he got the dye from, it had to be dyed, there was no way a beard could be that white, not without a touch of albinism, and white hair dye must be a specialist item.

"It's August, Mr. Claus." Smith remarked dryly.

"It's never too early for a touch of Christmas cheer."

"It decidedly is, Mr. Claus, and I'm afraid there isn't much cause for cheer today."

"We'll see about that, doctor."

We'll see indeed, thought Smith. It was wrong for a doctor to be thinking this way, it went against everything he'd trained for, this man was clearly ill, mentally and physically, but he was so unbearably smug, and even if he couldn't see it through the beard, the thought of wiping the smile from Santa's face was a darkly pleasing one.

"It's type two diabetes, Mr Claus."

"Ho ho ho no!"

Smith was suddenly struck with the urge to slap that stupid red hat off the man's head, how dare he crowbar a catchphrase into such a serious conversation, it was cheap, unnecessary and just proved how unstable he was. Smith took a deep breath and settled himself, Santa's mental instability had to take a back seat today, trying to solve his psychological problems would be a long and painful experience for both men, most likely ending in some sort of involuntary sectioning, and a lump of coal in Smith's stocking. But today was about Santa's physical health, and Smith would have to play along with his delusions, if only to help him in the short term.

"No more mince pies, Santa," Smith advised, trying to remain as earnest looking as he could, "now I understand you've lived a long life, although I have trouble believing that you're approaching two hundred, anyway, perhaps time can't kill you, but sugar certainly will."

"But you can't drink sherry without a mince pie or two, doc, that's just unreasonable."

"Mr Claus, you really ought to cut out the sherry as well. If I am to believe what you told me in our last appointment then on every Christmas Eve you drink enough sherry to kill an elephant, and enough mince pies to build a statue of one. That is simply unacceptable."

"Oh bah-humbug!" Came Santa's petulant retort.

He just had to fight through the next few minutes, but Smith was struggling to keep his cool here.

"You are going to die if you don't change your diet, Mr. Claus, no amount of festive spirit can cure diabetes, sir, and the longer you leave it untreated, the worse your health will become, I've seen people lose limbs to this disease." This was it, his last effort. Smith's mind was made up, if Santa didn't heed his advice now, he never would, and Smith would wash his hands of him.

"I'm not a rude man, doctor, and when the little boys and girls leave me treats I have to accept them, it's the polite thing to do."

Smith let loose an audible sigh this time, he could barely control his contempt for this man.

"You're a fool! Firstly, you're not the real Santa, he doesn't exist. Secondly, even if you were the real Santa, you're not immortal, your body is dying, and dying faster and faster with every candy cane and Christmas pudding you stuff down your fat gullet!"

Smith couldn't believe himself, this wasn't his normal behaviour, and it could land him on not just Santa's naughty list, but the NHS's as well. Strangely, Santa just sat there, it was unnerving, there was still an ignorant joy in his eyes and his ruddy cheeks were pinned back with a broad smile, it seemed almost evil. It occurred to Smith that he was just berating a mentally ill pensioner, but hell, he clearly didn't mind and Smith had a lot to get off his chest.

"You need to lose some weight, Claus! Maybe set the bloody sleigh down at the end of the street and jog between the houses you're so fond of breaking into. Perhaps you could release some of the elves you've bred into slavery and do some of the manual labour yourself. And you could always eat some of the carrots you bring in for the reindeers instead of gorging yourself on pigs in blankets seven days a week. Oh and stop flying that thing after drinking so much sherry, you might think you're invincible but one slip on the reins and your fleet of flying deer ploughs through an end terrace and kills a whole family. Buck your ideas up, dickhead!"

"Well... someone's not getting any presents this year."

"Good luck climbing down a chimney with an amputated foot."

"Oh sod you, Scrooge!" He shouted, and with that, Santa raised a hand, locked eyes with Smith and clicked his fingers. In a puff of smoke, he was gone. Disappeared. Maybe he was magic after all, thought Smith, but he left his insulin prescription behind, and magic or not, he wasn't going to get far without that.

The Pyre

by Stephen Jansen

It's a long drive to my version of Hell. It lives on a coastal town's sea front, mimicking a restaurant where tourists queue for hours to taste the five star food and the French champagne. Through tunnels cut into hills and ripped limestone escarpments I drive south west under rain and thunder skies with Bartok testing the suspension on the smooth road.

*

Here is my intended pyre. The black beams and bricks of the restaurant drip with water from the sprinklers and broiled strands of crystalline fat connect chairs to tables; the muscle and mucus dressed for dinner in charred rags. In the kitchen, chef bones are welded to charcoaled tiles and grill trays. The wrought iron gates and entrance ornaments are melted and twisted like toffee. Wine bottles are black and shattered by a row of fingers brazed to an ashtray. No survivors. My suit stinks of fresh smoke. I had fought for promotion. I had used a month's petrol driving to and from the restaurant to park my car and show my face; letting the management know I was in the area and eager to take the position. Sometimes fate blocks your path for a reason, like direct current travelling a wire and meeting a resistor that increases in power in proportion to the voltage. I failed the interview. Didn't get the job. Didn't move to the coast. I didn't die in the fire. My rival won; or lost, if you look at it that way. Hell has fates for all desires.

Father Christmas?

by Sam Arthur

It was the night of Christmas Eve, and the whole house had gone to bed. One person who could not sleep though was little Maisie, who was just too excited. She tried counting sheep in her head; but she could not get to sleep, she was just too excited. Maisie had no idea what she was going to get: she wanted a Panda, but her mum was not so sure about the idea.

Maisie tried for ages but could not get to sleep. She decided to go to the toilet, quickly rolling out of bed, and sneaking down stairs to the toilet. But on her way, she heard a noise coming from the lower floor. She thought nothing of it, until the noise got louder and louder. She needed the loo, but she decided to go and have a look downstairs too. Once again creeping quietly downstairs, she reached the bottom floor and heard the noise coming from the front room.

She walked up to the door, quietly turning the handle and walked in to see a big fat man wearing red and white clothing, carrying a bag over his shoulder.

"Father Christmas?" she spoke with a quiet wisp.

The big man in red and white with the bag over his shoulder turned around in surprise, to see young Maisie looking up at him. "Oh, hello little girl; shouldn't you be in bed right now?" he asked.

"I heard a noise while going to the toilet, what are you doing?" she probed further.

"Oh, erm, I'm delivering presents, it's what I do after all," the man replied.

"Why are you putting them in your bag from under the tree?" Maisie asked curiously.

The man looked at the tree, his big bag of presents, and then finally Maisie before reaching for his ear and touching it lightly.

"I'VE BEEN RUMBLED!" he shouted. He quickly dived for the chimney and hooked himself onto a wire before shouting to someone up the chimney, "QUICK; BEFORE THE FUZZ ARRIVE!"

Within seconds, he was pulled up the chimney, dragging his bag up with him.

Maisie walked over to the chimney and looked up in astonishment before saying "You forgot the milk and cookies I left for you."

The Christmas Special

by Mandy Pang

"Dude, maybe we should do this another night. Seems wrong, it's Christmas."

Phil is wishing desperately that Fenton will change his mind, but seeing his best friend's face harden, Phil knows he's wasting his time.

"No mate, I need this." Fenton had spent the last five years of this lousy festive season crowded around a tiny TV, in a pokey little high-rise flat, watching crap EastEnders specials with his grandma and granddad. Now they were no longer of this world, he wasn't giving this plan up for anything.

Tightening his sweaty grip around the ancient gun he took from his granddad's box of war memorabilia, he shoved the object and his hand deep into the pocket of his hoodie.

The shop was completely empty but for the bald, grey-bearded shop keeper. Fenton estimated his age to be around 68 years.

"Merry Christmas gentlemen," the shop keeper nodded in greeting.

"Alright, Merry Christmas to ya." Phil nodded back, but inside, his heart was about to leap out of his chest.

Fenton ignored them both and started picking up packets of crisps, turning them over with his one free hand as if he were checking the ingredients.

"He has allergies," Phil said to no one in particular as he stood next to Fenton. Nerves made Phil say things that didn't need to be said.

Something about the way the two teenage boys were acting made the shop keeper uneasy. Underneath the counter, he reached for his mobile phone and felt for the gun his wife had made him keep there.

"Not spending time with your family, gents? On a special night such as this, you should be with family." The shop keeper noticed how odd it was that the one with the hood was only using one hand.

What happened next appeared to Phil, as if it were occurring in ultra slow motion.

"Yeah, well why aren't you with *your* family?" Fenton was now right up next to the counter, pointing the gun at the shop keeper's head.

"Hands up in the air where we can see them old man." Images of him and Fenton drowning in a sea of lost souls burned in Phil's mind. They would surely go to hell for this.

"I don't want any trouble, especially not today." The police would take ages to get here, the shop keeper thought cynically.

"You know if you weren't so greedy, wanting to make money, you'd have closed up shop, and we wouldn't be standing where we are." Fenton was angry, really angry. It wasn't just adrenaline, it was something else. Weirdly, he thought he was going to start crying.

"Bet you're wishing you were with your family now hey?"

"Open the till mate, and put all the cash in this. Oh, and throw a couple of packets of Wine Gums in there too." Fenton looked at Phil in disbelief as Phil thew a Tesco carrier bag on the counter.

The shop keeper looked at them both and weighed up the situation in his head. Perhaps if he were a few years younger, he would be quick enough to duck under the counter and reach the gun in time. He wasn't scared, he had been threatened with all sorts in his time.

"Gentlemen, I will not be giving you away my money. I have worked hard for it. How about a few bottles of Vodka, and as many sweets as you like?" The shop keeper, with his arms still raised, kept a calm, even tone.

"Well…" Phil began, relieved they had an easy way out of this.

"Nah mate, I want the lot, and I'm prepared to pull the trigger for it."

"A murder, on Christmas day, are you sure you can live with this, young man? Such a waste of life don't you think?"

Fenton had had enough of this, the money was his way out of this boring, lifeless town. There were too many memories to hide from here.

"Christmas don't mean nothing to me anymore. You might wanna close you're eyes for this."

Phil watched open mouthed as Fenton squeezed the trigger.

And then… nothing happened. The gun had jammed.

"Grand Papa, are you closing shop soon? EastEnders is on in 20 minutes." At that very moment a young girl's voice called out from the back of the shop, and time sped up again.

"Fancy watching the EastEnders Christmas special gents? My wife made a trifle, and I think we have some red wine open?" The shop keeper looked at them, and then towards the back of the shop.

"Please mate, it's Christmas," Phil pleaded.

Finally realising he had picked the wrong fight, Fenton's shoulders fell.

"Yeah, that would be lovely," he said.

Finding Frank

by Nicholas McDonald

Frank Sullivan, the man was a legend back in the day. He was the bee's knees in the sales industry, and could sell sight to the blind, as they say, with relative ease. The women loved him, his colleagues adored him, and newcomers dreamed of being him. Good old Frank, he was incredible, and he knew it, there wasn't a mountain too high to climb.

That was then, this is now, and in his late eighties the bee's knees could barely stand on his. Life escaped Frank, and as he basked in his popularity, his financial success and handsome appearance, everyone got on with theirs and found their special someone, bought a home and started their own family. That was not the life for Frank, at least not at the time, but the day it became so, those he had close had gone and found their own journey, and as quickly as he could sell wings to a bee, he was all alone. His loneliness engulfed him, and eventually he became a recluse, getting by until his extreme wealth dwindled away, until all he owned was expensive cars and astonishing antiques. His loneliness became who he was, so he no longer felt the pain that came with it.

December had arrived, and Christmas proved to be his challenging foe, as he sat in his cold, dark home fantasising of the wife he never met, and his children he never had. The world had forgotten about Frank Sullivan, after all, you don't look for a shadow in a dark room. His only human interaction came when little Laura Frame passed him on the street, as her parents were out Christmas shopping. She had gotten lost in all of the hustle and bustle, her parents too lost in their schedule to realise she was no longer by their side.

Frank, sitting on the bench he always sat on, between 6 and 8pm—to ponder life and enjoy being in the company of others, even though they could care less of his existence, since even tightly knit villages can miss the most vulnerable of people—was joined by a tearful Laura Dunn. She sat on the bench sobbing, unaware of Frank.

"What's up little girl?"

She looked up at him, but could not speak through her tears.

"Are you lost?" His voice was smooth as silk and as warm as a sip of mulled wine.

Frank could see the fear in her eyes, realising that these days it was not safe for a child and an adult to speak if unacquainted. He sat back in his seat and smiled a smile that sold him over a million products in his lifetime

"I'm Frank. Frank Sullivan, you're safe here with me, there's no need to be upset. You're sad because you're lost now? I've been lost for the last forty years of my life. Here girl, take this napkin." He took a fresh white napkin from the inside of his left pocket and handed it to Laura. Her sobbing stopped and she used it to wipe her eyes.

"Thank you," she said, sweet as sugarcane, as a grin blossomed on her face. "I'm Laura Dunn."

"Pleasure to meet you, Laura," he said, tipping his flat-cap. "I suppose you're scared you've lost your parents?"

She nodded.

"Hmm, that's not very good. I bet you can't wait to find them straight away?"

"Yeah, what if they've forgotten me?"

Frank laughed gently, but stopped when he realised it was a very good fear to have, after all, the world had forgotten him.

"Here, Laura, take this." He took a mobile phone from his pocket and handed it to her, to which she accepted with a giant smile. "Give them a call, and tell them you're next to the giant Christmas tree. Then you can wait here until they come back."

"Okay, thank you, Mr…"

"Sullivan. But call me Frank."

"Okay, thank you, Frank."

She rang her parents, and they were ecstatic to hear her voice, explaining that they had been rushing around town in a panic looking for her, and they would meet her right away. In the meantime, she sat closer to Frank.

"Are you excited for Christmas, Frank?"

He sighed, and his eyes filled with tears unbeknown to him.

"Not anymore Laura."

"Why? Do you not have family?"

He chuckled.

"I don't, unfortunately." He looked at Laura, who was listening intently. "You see I have had many things, and done so very much, oh the stories I could tell. But you see, Laura, that feeling you have now, that need to have family and people around you?

41

Don't ever lose that. I have experienced a great many wonderful adventures, but the thing about stories and memories is that they're no good with no-one around to tell them to. My friends have moved on with their lives, and I never was able to fall in love, and in time, *I* am all that I have."

"Oh, but Frank, that's upsetting. You're a very lovely man, and you've made me feel safe."

"You're very sweet for saying so."

They sat in silence, enjoying the comfort of each others company until Laura's parents arrived. They thanked Frank for taking care of her and offered him a cash reward, to which he generously refused. The father recognised him as the old man who helps out at the Church, keeping it clean and looking after stalls, and joked that he said he saw him there that much, he could swear he lived there. Frank chuckled and explained he does not, but lives in the home at the very top of the hill they see before them; the big house: number 1. Mr Dunn laughed, as he told Frank that he thought nobody lived there, but Frank assured him he did. They said their farewells before Laura added, "Merry Christmas, Frank. Don't feel alone, I'll think about you."

Christmas Eve was soon on Frank's doorstep and he settled into his nightgown, put the fireplace on full and poured himself a glass of mulled wine. He was about to nod off at ten to midnight, when he heard the faintest of taps on the door; so faint he thought he'd imagined it.

Tap, tap… tap!

There it was again.

He struggled from his seat, his arthritis worsening at this time of year, and hobbled to the front door, picking up his walking stick along the way.

"Hello?"

But there had been no more tapping for the last minute.

"Who is it? Stop playing games!"

He continued to wobble towards the front door, and opened it, preparing himself for whatever trouble was beyond the door… Nothing.

He looked around outside, but there was no sign of anyone or anything untoward. It was only when he looked at the floor that he was a saw a piece of sugarcane on his doorstep. He picked it up to study it, then studied his driveway, where he saw another piece, and beyond that, a third sugarcane. Putting on his slippers and a thick jacket, Frank wandered along the driveway and onto the footpath, following the trail of sugarcanes. It went on and on, piece after piece, down the hill, past his local pub, the supermarket, the giant Christmas Tree, and all the way to the… Church. The lights were off, and the trail had finished. This was very peculiar, but he sensed that the purpose of the trail was to lead him to this very spot, and now that he had gotten this far, he may was well continue.

He opened the gate, and headed up the footpath to the large wooden doors, realising as he got closer, that the door was ajar.

He pushed it gently open and was about to call hello, when the lights switched on, and from the darkness appeared the entire village.

"Merry Christmas, Frank!" they yelled in unison.

"W-w-what? Eh?"

His throat was filled with a sudden lump, and his eyes with tears, but this time of happiness. However, he was still confused, until from the sea of happy faces appeared a little girl, Laura Dunn, with the face of an Angel and bearing a gift, to which she presented Frank. He opened it, seeing that it was journal.

"What's this for?"

"You've said you've got lots of stories. So I think you should write them down, and when I want to read something interesting, I'll open the book and enjoy one of yours."

"B-but why?"

"No-one should be alone for Christmas, Frank. And now you have all these people so you don't have to be unhappy. They're not for Christmas, they're for life."

And with the final statement, Frank found himself crying and embraced Laura with a huge hug, telling her how grateful he was.

The night was great fun, and as the morning crept upon all of the guests, Frank found himself next to a beautiful woman: Miss Frame from the local bakers. He hadn't seen her before but his heart throbbed when he set his eyes upon her.

He cleared his throat and stared into her incredible blue eyes, and with his winning smile he began.

"Hi, I'm Frank."

Inside the Mind of an Evil Fiction Writer

by Jean McDonald

Stephen was just an ordinary guy on the outside. Aren't they all? Blending in with the wallpaper, nodding a greeting as they pass and paying the milkman on a Friday.

But Stephen was quite an extraordinary chap. In his head existed an abundance of words and ideas vying with each other for a place at the front.

As a writer of fictional evil, he needed this lexicon store to earn his crust. Having a natural talent for seeing the dark side of things, he wrote avidly about evil doings.

He had enjoyed a good few horror writing years, finding freelance consultancy work in the theatre, which brought in a steady income.

However, Christmas was approaching quickly, a feast of do-gooding, merry cheering and the like, and the thoughts he had did not fit in with Santa's message and the Babe in a manger.

Stephen wanted to think good thoughts during the season of angelic beings and goodwill and he was concerned he might now have lost the magic.

It was twilight and Stephen was leaning back in his chair, his feet on the desk, when he noticed a movement through the open back door, he could see there was a sinister stranger in the chicken coop. The light from his office did not extend totally as far as the chicken coop so he switched on the torch that he kept in his desk, but the flat batteries made him tut.

He lit a nearby candle on the gas cooker and made his way down the garden. "Oh no, here we go again" he thought as the snow began to fall and choristers sang gaily at the end of the road. Merry Christmas!

The Christmas Market

by Persis Peters

"I say, listen here. Don't you know who I am? Major Armstrong of the 1st Fairground Battalion, that's who. 'Strong arm' by name, 'strong arm' from holding this blasted candy cane for 24 days straight. I survived an onslaught of Waitbury's Extra Finest mince pies yesterday so you needn't think that throwing your dirty bag of unfinished chips at me will cause me to falter. What's that you say? I'm a Christmas Cracker joke. Oh, I'll give you a 'joke'. Oi. Stop it. My hat is not an ashtray. Ah, blue flashing lights! That's it, run away. Cowards.

"I beg your pardon, Sergeant Starrett? I can assure you those blue lights were NOT the Wurlitzers in the park. When a military man is in trouble the police will come.

"ON GUARD! Officers approaching. Atterrrhhhn-SHUN.

"Excuse me Officer but are you sure this isn't highly irregular? Some may say I'm made of wood but I'm not on fire and I'm certain it's a *fireman's* hose you would need in such a situation. And why is your truncheon wrapped in tinsel? Oh, goodbye then. What? Don't be silly, Starrett. That's not an office party; they had handcuffs and everything.

"It is quiet tonight, Starrett. Where is everyone? The wine is being mulled in the mess and the horses are saddled and ready to go.

"Ah, here they come. Remember, Starrett, children like surprises. Don't let on you're not a toy soldier until the very end."

The Present
by Maya Anna Ozolina

I knew straight away that the present was for me. I bet it was not here when I walked in our 'big room', as we call it, a short while ago.

It wasn't wrapped, just a white bag with an appliqué red tulip on it.

"Strange", I thought, "Why is it not wrapped?"

Anyway, I'll find out soon, just a little while to wait.

The table was set and everything was ready.

My mum invited everybody to take a seat around the table and the feast started.

As usual, there were lots and lots of different foods, and lemonade for us children, but my eyes were more on the white bag under the tree than on all the treats on the table.

It looked like the bag moved a little. Yes, it moved! No, it didn't, it couldn't, I must be too excited.

Finally, grandma said, "Time for presents!"

My dad took his place next to the Christmas tree to give out the gifts; you see we did not have a Father Christmas or anything like him.

To get your present, you had to perform—that's the tradition, there was no way out of it. All the children were prepared, equipped with poems, songs and even jokes, all learned by heart. My dad was strict, for each present everybody had to perform.

I loved performing; I could not wait. Sometimes I even performed in place of my mum and grandma, so they didn't have to.

Dad picked up the white bag and said, "This present must go first. Maya, it's for you!"

Before I could open my mouth, the bag fell over and a rabbit jumped out of it.

Oh, my word, I never had a pet rabbit, my heart nearly jumped out of my chest, like the rabbit from the bag.

Unfortunately the rabbit had to go and live with the chicken in the shed, but on a good note he had his own little house my dad built for him.

Every day, I went to wish the rabbit good morning and good night, I got him out on the lawn, played and talked to him—my Christmas rabbit.

No wonder those were the first Christmas memories I remembered clearly. I was 4 then, I think.

Chocolate Memories

Iveta Kraule

The old cardboard box is touched just once a year, when the shopping madness has started and the Coca Cola train has arrived. No need to guess, it's Christmas time.

Left in a dark wardrobe, the box is waiting very patiently for a chance to be opened. Gathering dust from all around, deformed from dampness, but very reliable for me. Every item inside, one by one, is a small piece of my childhood.

The first decoration that catches my eye is Snow White, made from porcelain, shiny and fragile. I remember my duty was to be an assistant for my Dad, who was the main Christmas tree decorator. Silver cones, simple white candles and walnuts painted in gold. Kitsch is a style, isn't it?

I am hanging all the decorations on a stylish but artificial Christmas tree—no scent, no feelings.

Suddenly a glossy chocolate paper shines in my eyes. It is a big chocolate sweet in a bright blue wrapper with long, white paper fringes at both ends. I open it. There is cotton wool inside. Memories run like lightening through my head. I remember myself, with a sweet tooth, secretly opening all the chocolates and being scared to be caught, then stuffing the wrappings with cotton wool afterwards. When Dad realised what I'd done, he never said a word to me.

Dad, I miss you so much! I know you are a star in the sky looking down to me.

Merry Christmas, wherever you are!!!!

The Spirit of Christmas

by Susan Moffat

T'was late Christmas Eve and the turkey was dressed,
The children were shiny, Dad needed a rest.

He'd peeled the potatoes, ahead of the day,
He'd done all the washing and put it away.

He'd helped write the lists and he'd put up the tree
He'd re-watched The Grinch every time he was free.

He carried his babies upstairs to their beds,
And read them a story to weary their heads.

He tucked them both in and he kissed them goodnight
And closed the door over and prayed they'd stay tight.

He sat on the staircase until they both slept
Then slowly downstairs to the kitchen he crept.

He made himself coffee, prepared for the wait
And dozed in the armchair, T'was already late.

Then from the front doorway he heard such a clatter
He leapt from the chair to see what was the matter,

And there by the light of the bright winter moon
Stood Mum, home from work not a minute too soon.

She carried an armful of goodies and things
With stickers of yellow and some tied with strings,

She laid them all out on the table to see
What bargains she'd bagged on this cold Christmas Eve.

Dad made her hot chocolate and soon they both snoozed,
Curled up on the sofa in front of the news.

They didn't see Santa come into the room
With armfuls of presents to brighten the gloom,

He took all the bargains and put in their place
A bounty of treasures, and left not a trace

Of stickers of yellow and boxes with strings.
Instead he left marvellous, sparkling things.

And as they awoke from their short Christmas sleep
They vowed that the wonder of Christmas they'd keep,

It's not what you spend that keeps Christmas alive,
It's the spirit of love that helps magic thrive.

About the Authors

The writers who contributed to this book are all members of the *Just Write* group, based in Preston, Lancashire, in the UK. We are united by a love of writing and are excited to share some of our work with you at this special time of year.

As you can tell by the stories, we have varied writing styles and recognise that Christmas means many different things to different people.

But what we have in common is a love of telling stories, and we hope you enjoyed reading them as much as we did creating them.

Your authors, in alphabetical order, are:

Sam Arthur	samstoriesblog.wordpress.com/
Nusantara Banget-Rani	
Matthew Bennett	matthewjohnbennett.tumblr.com
Arthur Chappell	www.mylot.com/arthurchappell
Janice Cumberlidge	janicecumberlidge.com
Leanne Dempsey	instagram.com/miss_leanne_d
Karen Howarth	
Stephen Jansen	deadliner@hotmail.co.uk
Iveta Kraule	facebook.com/iveta.kraule.3
Jean McDonald	jeanin30@aol.com
Nicholas McDonald	nick_black92@aol.com
Susan Moffat	smoffat99.wordpress.com
Maya Anna Ozolina	facebook.com/maya.a.ozolina
Mandy Pang	mandypang.co.uk
Persis Peters	persispeters.com
Jake Trusler	twitter.com/JakeTrusler

Thanks for reading, it would mean a lot to us if you would leave a review!

Printed in Great Britain
by Amazon